Text & illustrations copyright © 2019 Robert Forsyth

All right reserved.

BILLY
AND THE
FRUITY FOX

Written by

Robert Forsyth

Illustrated by

Ambadi Kumar

The sky was grey. Thunder rumbled,

and rain crashed against the window.

Billy – who was just a puppy – was fast asleep,

gently snoring as he lay by his favourite window.

Suddenly the lightning flashed so very brightly

and the thunder clapped so very loudly

that Billy woke with a start.

Billy stared at the window, his eyes wide with fright.

The thunder crashed again and the lightning flashed again,
lighting up the whole sky.

Billy yelped and barked, running and hiding under the table
before covering his eyes with his paw.

He lay there for a very long time,
and eventually he began to feel sleepy again.

Before long he was fast asleep, dreaming of his favourite
bone that lay outside in the garden.

By the time Billy woke from his nap,

the storm had passed.

He yawned and stretched,

then he went to his favourite place by his favourite window.

He looked for his bone, smiling when he saw it

lying in the garden, just where he'd left it. However...

There was a fox standing in the garden!

Billy immediately stopped smiling and began to growl.

He ran to the back door of the house,

and upon finding it open, he ran straight out into the garden.

Deciding to sneak up on the fox, Billy began crawling quietly along

the pathway, hidden by the bushes and shrubs.

Billy crawled until he reached the fox, then he barked so loudly

that the fox jumped high into the air,

landing a second later on the soft grass and shaking with fright.

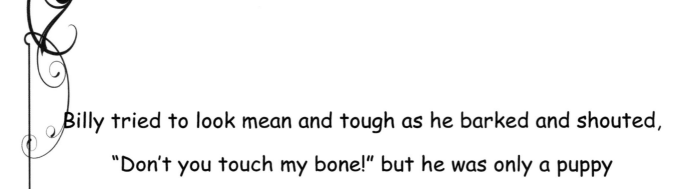

Billy tried to look mean and tough as he barked and shouted, "Don't you touch my bone!" but he was only a puppy and his voice came out all squeaky.

The fox was very young too. He stared at Billy and said in a very soft voice, "I don't like bones, I like fruit. Strawberries are my favourite."

Billy couldn't help but laugh. "Foxes don't eat fruit," he said, "They catch chickens and rabbits for dinner!"

The fox smiled and softly replied, "Well, I'm different." Billy tilted his head to one side, and then to the other.

The fox continued, "In fact, some of my best friends are chickens and rabbits."

Billy relaxed then, and knowing that his bone was safe, he stopped trying to look mean and tough.

In fact, he started to wag his tail and exclaimed excitedly, "My name is Billy, and I can be your friend too – we can play in the garden if you like!"

The fox jumped very high in the air, and when he landed he said softly, "I'd like that very much. You can call me Foxy."

That afternoon, Billy and Foxy played together in the garden.
They rolled in the grass and ran up and down the lawn,
going back and forth until they were both very tired.

They got very thirsty too, so when Billy saw a puddle next to
a vegetable patch, he took a big drink from it.
Foxy, however, didn't want any water.

He had spotted some big juicy strawberries in the vegetable
patch, and as he licked his lips he said to Billy,
"Do you think I could have one of those lovely red strawberries?"

Billy looked at the strawberries and said,
"Yes, they're just lying around the garden.
I don't think anyone will mind."

So, Foxy ate one of the strawberries, and then he
and Billy lay under a tree to have a nice, cosy nap.

After their nap Foxy said sleepily, "I have to go home now. My mother worries when I stay out too long."

Billy walked with Foxy until they reached the hedgerow, and after peering through a gap in the hedge, Foxy froze.

Billy started to speak but Foxy suddenly hissed, "Shhhh!" Billy poked his head through a gap in the hedge too, asking in a whisper, "What's wrong, Foxy? You look worried."

Foxy turned to Billy and said very quietly, "I can see one of the older foxes through there. He's a bad tempered old fox, and he's after the chickens in that garden."

Billy could see them too, and with his eyes wide

with alarm he exclaimed, "He wants those chickens for his

dinner!" Foxy nodded.

"We have to save them, Billy – those chickens are my friends!"

So, Billy and Foxy made a plan

and started putting it into action.

Foxy moved around one side of the garden,

while Billy moved around the other side.

Foxy could see an empty washing basket on top of a

big tree stump. The old fox was crouched beside the tree

stump, ready to pounce on the unsuspecting chickens.

Foxy ran and jumped very high, crashing into the empty

washing basket and knocking it over.

The basket landed right on top of the old fox,

trapping it underneath.

Then Billy and Foxy worked together,

rounding up all the chickens.

They guided them back into the chicken house

and closed the door, securing the chickens safely inside.

Billy and Foxy went to the window of the chicken house,

explaining to the startled chickens what had happened.

Foxy's friends thanked them for their help,

and Foxy replied in his very soft voice,

"That's what friends do, they help each other.

And if we see others who need our help,

we'll try to help them too."

Billy and the chickens knew that Foxy was different,

but it didn't stop them from being friends.

Foxy might be different, but he was also kind, thoughtful,

and caring. In fact, they thought Foxy was really quite special.

Billy and Foxy said goodbye to the chickens.

They said goodbye to each other too,

but they promised to meet again the very next day.

The End

Printed in Great
Britain
by Amazon